GREGORY SANDERS

authorHOUSE®

AuthorHouse™
1663 Liberty Drive
Bloomington, IN 47403
www.authorhouse.com
Phone: 1 (800) 839-8640

Published by AuthorHouse 12/16/2015

ISBN: 978-1-4772-8339-4 (sc)
ISBN: 978-1-4772-8343-1 (e)

Library of Congress Control Number: 2012919880

Contents

Kelly's Story

It is late at night and Kelly comes home and goes into the bathroom after a day's work. While she is in the bathroom she looks into the mirror for a brief moment. While she is looking at the mirror she then stares into the mirror and goes into a trance like stare. She then reaches for a bottle of aspirin she thinks about it as she does every night she thinks of doing it today, this is it I'm going to do it, I'm really going to do it, like every other day she just puts the pills back into the bottle and say to herself it was just a thought. Kelly is not able to go through with it. She can't kill herself, so she just walks away and gets ready for bed. It is an everyday experience that lots of people are dealing with. A secret that is so horrible sometimes they have to pull over and take time to deal with it however they chose to deal with it. Kelly thinks back to when she was a young girl about 10 or 12 years old, she was always playful, more than other kids that were her age. It was like that for a while, until that day when she first met her Uncle Terry, who is her father's younger brother. At first Uncle Terry, as she would come to call him, was very friendly. He gave her everything she wanted and if he could get it, it was hers. After a while he got to a point where he even started to separate her from her friends. That's when he started to make a move. Slowly, but cautiously he suddenly began to touch her in ways that she felt was funny and made her uncomfortable. He then began to do it more without even a care and Kelly began to become extremely uncomfortable. It was that way until, one day he lurned her over to his apartment and then it happened. He lured her to the back room and while they were talking he began to make a pass at her. Suddenly, he pulled her over to him and laid her across the bed. He then began to rip her clothes off and you know the rest. After it was over and Kelly was lying there covered in blood and crying. He then began begging her not to say anything to her parents but, she said she was going to tell her parents. He stood up and walked around in a circle and then began to plead with her, but she insisted that she was going to tell. Terry then stood up and smiled and said "Go ahead. Tell them. So who do you think your father will believe, you a worthless ass little girl or me, his own little brother whom he has known since childhood?" Terry continued by saying how it would just kill her mother if she knew what kind of slut she is. Kelly then went back down stairs and cleaned herself up and changed clothes with her Uncle Terry's help. Of course, this went on for years. Terry would continue to touch her over and over again until one day, he just stopped. To Kelly the nightmare went on and on, until Kelly noticed her younger aunt's daughter started to come around her Uncle Terry. Does this sound familiar? This is why some young people often do poorly in school, as well as get into fights along with selfless issues. Sometimes we have to look at why these problems exist. According to the National Child Abuse Statistics, believe it or not, this is about 7.6 of the incidents that occur to our children and 30 percent carry on the cycle by doing the same thing to their children when they get older.

Mark's Story

It is late at night, and Mark, twelve years, is up trying not to cry because if he did cry, his mother would wonder what has happened. Why her baby is crying. He would have to tell her and the bad guy would hurt mommy. This guy that he is referring to is, he is mother's boyfriend Carl. Carl was a friendly and charismatic young man. He had a smile that could charm a baby out of a milk bottle. Mark, her son, would feel like he could talk to Carl about anything in the world, because Carl made him feel that way. Carl would also do anything he could for him. It was that way until one day he and Carl were alone playing and Carl said to mark, "I bet you won't take your shirt off." As they were playing, Mark replied "I bet I will." That was the worst mistake that Mark could have made. After that, Carl took his shirt off and said to Mark, "I bet you won't kiss me." Mark at first felt that something was wrong, but he did it anyway. As Mark was leaning over to kiss Carl, he suddenly grabbed Mark, pulled him into him and he snatched his pants off and said "If you don't say anything, I won't hurt your mother. Do you hear me?" At first Mark did not say anything, and then Carl said "Do you hear me?" "Yes" replied Mark, as he laid there in shock. Carl then stood up and pulled down his pants. You know the rest. When he finished, Mark had gotten up and ran into the bathroom to rinse out his mouth. Mark could not get over what Carl did. He wanted to tell his mother, but he was afraid to. This story often happens to girls. What people don't know is that boys are victims of rape far more than they expect. Carl came over to visit Mark's mother a couple more times. Each time Carl came over, Mark would become nervous even when his mother would tell him to go speak to Carl. Sometimes Mark would speak, but he would still be nervous. It happened a few more times. Then Carl suddenly left Mark and his mother alone, but each time he came over, and including the last time, he warned mark not to say anything, or he would hurt his mother. Mark's mother noticed that Mark would often get into fights at school. She would often get calls from school about his class work and his homework. These are some of the symptoms of child sex abuse that 5 percent of the child abuse.

I Love Him

It is late at night and Jenifer, is sitting there wondering about how she can keep her boyfriend. Jennifer is a normal fifteen year old high school student who is slightly on the cute side. She is dating Michael, a tenth grader at Fairbank's High School. The two have been dating for a few months. He is a little rough looking and also a bully. That doesn't seem to matter to her. She is uncontrollably attracted to him and she seems to not mind him bullying or acting tough with people now and then. This seems to make her feel secure from the other bullies around the school. She was alright with it until the day for her to be bullied by him. It stated the same as the others. Jennifer was busy getting ready for school when her phone started to ring. She looked at the phone's caller id and saw it was Michael. She was in a hurry and said *"I will see him at school later."* She then finished getting her things together and off to school she went. Upon arriving at school she asked his friends where was he. One of them said he saw him around by the cafeteria, so she went over to the cafeteria. It was sad that she did not know that she was being set up. Jennifer saw Michael talking to another girl, and they were not just talking like people talk to one another, it seemed suspicious. She asked Michael, "Who is this girl you are talking to?" Before she knew it, Michael had turned around and had his finger pointing in her face. Michael told Jennifer "Don't be coming up in my face confronting me like that, especially when I called you and you didn't have time to see what I wanted." Jennifer said "Get your finger out of my face." Michael then slapped Jennifer in the face twice to let her know that she was being disrespectful. A small crowd stood around and started to laugh at her as her eyes swelled with tears. She then ran away into the girl's restroom where she finished crying. Later that day, Michael approached her and started to apologize to her for hitting her, but she had it coming, he said. They talked about it and later they got back together. They are still together and every now and then there would be a misunderstanding between the two. All it would take is a slap in the face by Michael and some talking to and they would get back together. These types of domestic abuse among teenagers go on in high schools across the nation. It is not clear what actually the cause of the abuse is. Some say that the abuse is hereditary and passed on from generation to generation.

I Don't Care

It is late at night and Nick is excited about meeting Sarah and boy was she a good looking girl. The fact that she was even considering talking to him would make his day. For this thirteen year old who most people considered kind of geeky looking and weird. This did not bother him because he had the most beautiful girl in the world that was going to be talking with him shortly. The time came for Nick to call Sarah, and when Nick did, he felt like this was finally the one that he had dreamed of being with. Their conversation was then over for the night. The next day Nick was dressed up due to his conversation the night before. He was looking for Sarah, but was not able to find her. At first he did not think anything of it. He just went on his way looking for Sarah, but it was no success.

That evening when they were talking, he asked her where she was today when he came to school and Sarah laughed and changed the conversation. The next day when he came to school he was looking for Sarah again and once more she avoided him. Watching him looking around for here and no avail he just could not find her. It was obvious to Nick that she was playing with him and she did not care anything about him or his feelings. When he called her later on that evening, he could hear voices in the background telling someone that she was just playing with him like she was going with him just to make a fool out of him, while she had the phone pressed against her chest. She was not aware that he was listening. When she found out that he was listening, at first she was shocked, but then she finally mustered up enough courage to say to him, "Look I don't care anything about you or your feelings. I was just playing with you." Suddenly, she hangs up on him without saying anything else. Nick is badly hurt and devastated. He was just trying to be her friend and possibly, her boyfriend. He was not the most popular boy in school. He knew this, but what he could not understand is why would she do this to him? How could she just hurt him like that? This type of abuse is very common; it is an emotional abuse that most young people do daily to one another. Why do they like treating one another's emotions like it is a game? There is not one answer. They hurt one another by playing games like this. Just remember that what goes around comes around.

I Am Abused

It is late at night; Ray would lay there and think about how hard it was when he was seven years old. That is when it all happened, the physical abuse that he would suffer, the abuse that would last a life time and put a strain on him and his mother's relationship. Ray often would think back to the day when he first met his mother's boyfriend Dave. He seemed ruthless from the beginning. It was when Ray had turned ten years old that he saw Dave's other side. When Ray came into the kitchen where Dave was smoking a cigarette, He asked where his mother was. She is gone to the store answered Dave. Ray then told Dave that he was going outside over a friend's house to play. When Dave interrupted him talking and told "*Shut up, no you cannot go,*" at first Ray thought that Dave was just playing, that was until Dave started yelling at him, "*Go to your room, NOW do you hear me?*" Ray thought that Dave was playing, until Ray pulled off his belt and grabbed Ray by his collar, and told him "*I said go to your room, I am not playing with you. Do you hear me?*" Dave then struck him with the belt and shoved Ray away from him. He went into the front room . . . Later when Ray' mother came home Dave talked to her about something. Then Ray's mother came into Ray's room and told him that he should apologize to Dave for how he acted. "*How do I owe him an apology when all I was asking him was could I go outside and play,*" said Ray. Then Ray looked at his mother in disbelief. He was in shock when she said this. As time went by, Ray like most young people, forgot about it and he was letting by gone be by gone. Until another day came when Ray's mother had gone to the store and she left Dave to babysit Ray when he came home from school. As Ray entered the house, he saw Dave and asked him could he go to the candy house to get some candy. That's when Dave slapped Ray in the mouth and began yelling and cursing him out for no reason at all. Ray then got up and ran to his room, shut and locked the door until his mother came home. Dave once again was already talking to Ray's mother when Ray entered the room. After a few more minutes, she had told Ray to go get a belt and give it to Dave. Ray hesitated, but then he got the belt and gave it to Dave. She then told Dave to whip his little butt until he can't sit down. Dave did just what Ray's mother said. Ray tried to plea with his mother, but she would not listen. Ray often argued with his mother when they were alone, and they would often fight amongst themselves about Dave, but what Ray doesn't understand is that his mother loves Dave no matter how he is and she feels that Ray should give him a chance. That is why so many of our children in the United States often get involved in fights in school and have problems trusting people and often are runaways . . . This is about 10.8 to 11 percent of the children in America. This is slightly the ones who are sexually abused children.

Tony

It is late at night and Tony is walking up to Lisa's house. He is getting ready to pick up his nine year old daughter Lisa, fro over her mother's house, for his weekend visit. Sometimes when he picks her up, she sits there and don't say anything. Then there are times that she is somewhat talkative, but she is mostly quiet. Finally one day he came to pick her up and while she was sitting there he asked her, "What's wrong?" At first Lisa did not want to say anything, but hen softly she said, "My mother whoops me, I talk too much." "What are you talking about," then there was nothing. As she visits her father and his family she would mostly sit there, even if she wanted to play, she would sit there and do nothing. Sometimes when Tony drops her off, she would ask him with tears in her eyes if she could go back with him, but he have to tell her no. Not because he did not want her, but because that was part of the custody battle. Lisa then wiping the tears from her eyes got out of the car and slowly went to the door. While tony was driving away he looked back in his rear view mirror. He sees Joy, yelling at her. Lisa would stand there looking as if she was crying. The door shut and he would not know anything until next weekend. That was the weekend he finally asked her what was going on. She didn't know what to say so she just sat there until they got to his house. Tony then took Lisa to the back room of his home where Lisa started crying. He asked her again, this time he asked her in a soft and reassuring way. "What happened Lisa, you can tell your father if no one else." Lisa leaned in to cry in her father's arms and the back of her shirt slightly revealed her back.

Tony then saw what he suspected all alone, a bruise. At first he saw one, and then he looked again and saw bruises along her leg and back. Yes, it's unfortunate. Lisa was being abused all because Tony was not interested in marrying her mother, Joy. Tony did take care of his responsibility. Lisa was paying the price for it. This kind of abuse happens to children every day across America.

Mark

It is late at night and Mark is looking out of the window. His eyes are gone into a deep stare and he's looking off and thinking back to the time when he was just eleven years old. When his mother, who he loved very much, was hooked on drugs and often was gone for days at a time. It did not bother him at first. Whenever she would return home it was only for a few minutes and off she would go. When she would come home to stay a while, Mark would try to talk with her about her drug problem. She would not say anything to him about it. Off she would go from one dope house to another spending her money up getting high. She then offered her body for sexual favors, spending the money on drugs, and she would sell anything she could get her hands on. This is common for about six hundred million of our children in America that most of the parents are on drugs. Some of our children are left to raise themselves. Not because the children want to raise themselves, but they have no choice. He doesn't know how to raise his little brother and sister, because they are too young for him. Mark could have done more if only he knew how to ask for help. They would often get into fights with other kids at school and in the neighborhood for talking about their mother. Sometimes they would have to steal food so they could eat. They would do anything short of sleeping around in order to survive. There would be times that they would go to the school without taking a bath even for a few days at a time, or they wouldn't change clothes sometimes for days. They had a problem getting along with their friends when they were not fighting. Mark would often wonder what he could have done to help his mother from turning to drugs. Or at least talk with somebody about what was wrong. Was it the peer pressure? Whatever the reason, they needed their mother, and their mother just wanted to get high. Whatever the reason, she just was not close to them, and did not want them getting close to her. Most parents like this don't care about their children, just getting high is all they want. Mark grew up and often he would have to shake off the hate and teasing by the other children in the neighborhood, laugh at his mother and him for trying to help her. Sometimes, he even would miss school to help her get off of drugs. Mark was determined to get his mother the help she needed. It was often to no avail. She would just walk out of the facility. She was sprung and that simply means she is going to keep doing drugs no matter what. Mark still would try to do whatever he could to get her off of drugs. She would start, but as usual she would just walk out. This is still going on, but none the less, after eight years, he's still trying. Mark would then come out of the stare and light up a joint and walk off shaking his head as he prepares to takes his mother to rehab. It is not unusual for a person to use drugs after being exposed to it. What can be done to stop drug abuse? Go to drug rehab or just simply form a support group. Those are simple ideas that might work.

Alvin's Story

It is late at night and Alvin is on his way home. Alvin is one of the highest ranking students at the local high school. He is always there early in the morning, and always willing to stay late in the afternoon to finish his homework assignment. Yes, things are looking good for Alvin academically, but not so much on the financial side. You see he's also one of the worst dressed of students that attend there too. What everybody doesn't know about Alvin, is that when he goes home it is a different story for him. You see Alvin hides a secret like three percent of the children in America. His brother Ralph, six years old and his sister Ellen, five years old were abandoned. That is bad enough, Alvin is the oldest. Each morning Alvin gets his siblings Ralph and Ellen, up early and they go over to the local convenience store. They wash up and put on their clothes the best they can. They then hurry off to school. You see, their mother is always gone and when she does come home, she brings home some strange man with her, who looks at and treats Alvin, his brother, and sister like dirt. He would tell Alvin's mother to get rid of them so they could be alone. There were times when Alvin and his siblings would stay out and have to sleep in an alley that was in the back of the house, while Alvin's mother entertained her company inside of their home. Alvin's mother is an alcoholic. It does not meant that is an excuse for what she is doing, but it offers some kind of reason to why she is never home, or do anything for them when she is there. A lot of neighbors would sometimes let Ralph and Ellen stay over to their homes. Every now and then that was a big help to them. Although, Alvin was invited to stay there if he wanted to, he already had some place he could stay. It was over one of his friend's house, Albert. There still was a problem, whenever she was at home, she would be so drunk that sometimes she could stand up, or talk straight without mumbling her words or stumbling over something. She does not seem to be embarrassed or bothered about her excessive drinking. It clearly bothers Alvin and his siblings, who doesn't like it one bit. Whenever they would try to tell their mother about their accomplishments in school, most of the time she would just fall asleep or if she is awake, she was just too drunk to care. Some days, Alvin would find it easier to stay in school as long as possible or even stay over his friend Albert's house and spend the night if possible. Afterwards he would get his brother and sister somewhere they could stay. It it was not for his brother and sister, Alvin probably would have run away. He is waiting until he gets old enough to get custody of them. This is a form of abuse. Like I said, three percent of the children live this life every day. You have examples of parents leaving their children behind; to face abuse to find for themselves is a form of abuse. These children are more than likely to get arrested both as juveniles and as adult. The children have to learn at an early age to care for themselves and to survive.

Katrina

It is late at night and Katrina's mother is up and looking about for her clothes that she is going to wear in the morning, while Katrina follows alongside her mother. This happens every day for this ten year old, that has no friends. Her mother does not trust what few relatives they have. They move around from place to place. Only because she and her mother do not stay in one place long enough to make any friends. This also affected her in school being that she was not there a lot of times. Sometimes she wonders why her life is the way that it is. She wondered if she could live a normal life. "How come I can't go to school? I feel like I can learn like others can." She would always ask herself these and other questions like these. This sometimes was embarrassing to her, but to this ten year old, it was just of life. Katrina spends much of her time looking through garbage's for food, clothes. The streets are not easy to live on, there are times when Katrina and her mother are lucky enough to get into a shelter for the night. Katrina and her mother have been alone for the last two years. Every time the subject came up about letting Katrina live with relatives, her mother would become enraged so that Katrina would rather not bring it up and just let it go. Since her father left them when he got arrested for drugs, they were evicted from their small apartment. Her mother sometimes struggle with herself about having to give Katrina up, but she doesn't because she doesn't have anybody and she just cannot face this alone. So against her better judgment, she keeps Katrina and they will weather through this storm somehow. Time went by and Katrina was growing and with it came developing in all the right places. One day a stranger came up to Katrina. He was rough looking and kind of perverted looking as well. He told her that he would give five dollars if she would let him, you know the rest. Katrina told him no and left the area immediately. Later on she told her mother about it. Her mother looked at her and said calmly, "there are times when men will look at you and they will have nasty thoughts on their minds. You have something that they want, between your legs. You already know what it is. You can control the way they act towards you. If you know how to make them do what you want them to do. All you have to do is go in there look at the walls, brace yourself, and in a few minutes it will be over with." Years have gone by and Katrina is no longer the shy quiet little girl she once was. Katrina is now twenty-three years old, a mother of two children, one five years old and the other two years old. Her education level is somewhat lacking as well as her high genes and loks, yes the years she spent on the streets under educated because of the lack of school, having to take jobs for less pay, alone with drug abuse and even having to prostitute herself so they could make a living. Yes, it took it's toile on Katrina, and her mother. This is often what happens to the homeless, not all of them; about 5 percent of the homeless children have this problem. It is estimated that over one hundred million children are homeless world-wide and probably live like this.

Earnest

It is late at night, and Earnest and his family are moving out again on a midnight move. A midnight move is when you cannot make a payment and your rent is due real soon. Then you wait until night and move somewhere else before management can catch up with you. Earnest as I said earlier, did not like the way he and his family moved from time to time. All he ever wanted was to live in a nice home with a front yard he could play in, but all his father ever told him was that they would have to more. Eventually they would have to m one move off to another neighborhood and school, where he would make friends all over again. This would happen again and again. Earnest was tired of this constant moving and finally one day, Earnest ran away. Was he running away because he got tired of being laughed at or because he was chasing a dream? This is something that is ongoing with America's kids. There are children like Earnest in America that every day they are living in poverty. It is no wonder that children are always angry. They don't have anything and when they do see people with something, the people then turn on them with the intent of bragging about their accomplishments. The American dream idea of working hard and you can get something out of it. This is nothing but a lie, people really believe it and buy into it, but often have nothing to show for it. That is what the kids are seeing everyday they would see this someone buying into the American dream but to no avail. That is why a lot of American children are so angry.

Samantha

It is night time elsewhere and Melvin is on the streets in the city looking around at every car that drives by. When a driver would give him a nod he would nod back and tell them to meet him in the ally. Cautiously he would approach the car and make the drug deal. That is how this nineteen year old, makes his living for the past five years. Since his father abandoned him and his mother for a woman that was younger and a little more attractive than his mother. This is also how he supports his family. This time he sold to an undercover police officer again. This was nothing unusual it is part of the game. Again, he would have to call Sam, that is the nickname he calls his girlfriend, whose real name is Samantha. She would come and bail him out. That was how it usually goes; until Sam could not get him out of jail due to the fact he could not make bail. He was going to be there for a while and rent on their apartment was due in a week from now. Sam or Samantha had to find work and fast. She knew a local pimp, Raul, who had the money, but she had to pay him back one way and one way only. So she would go every day and work the streets to make some money. The problem is that Sam did not tell her John's that she was only seventeen years old. This is true about seven hundred thousand teenage girls in America. They are trying to survive making ends meet, and they do this sometimes in the name of love. The one thing they did not get at home. Why is it that most teenager girls feel that they did not find love at home? Sometimes they are just hard headed and don't want to mind their parents, or could they have been abused. Either way there is something wrong and love could possibly be the answer. What about Melvin, and his drug dealing. How is this going to work out with him and his constantly getting arrested? We don't really know we just have to hope for the best. Like most children in America.

I Am Gone

It is late at night, where Jennifer is getting ready for bed. She stops every now and then and think back to when she was eight years old. That is the day that her mother left. She just up and left without saying goodbye or offering any reasons. Her mother did have a reason, it might not have been a good reason, it was the best she could come up with. She just did not want to be a mother anymore. She just walked away from it. For now we focus on the young women, they are the ones who will be the o another generation of children. We have to try to find a way them from getting pregnant and giving them that motherly love hey need. Therefore, it is important to try to find out what is driving r mothers away from them. August 29, 2012 article in Oregon Women Report mainly states that 'There is no reason why mother's walk out on kids.' What can be done to stop this walking out of kids by their mother's? What affect does this walking out on them have? It feels to them like they did something or perhaps they said something and there is no way to make it right. There are many kids that feel this way, but truthfully they should not feel like this, it is not their fault. This abandonment may cause mental disorder, a problem such as self image, behavior problems, personality disorders, and more. Sometimes they dress inappropriately, absent from school and the need for attention also contributes to the lack of parents not being there. There is assistance for these children as it is for other children of abuse. Such as talking to someone, anyone that they can get to listen to them, whatever the reason are their mothers abandoned their children and leave. Whatever the reason, Jennifer just shrugs her head and tells herself that she would never be like her mother. Jennifer then leans over into a crib, picks up her daughter, and walks into the next room while wiping tears from her eyes. The reason why her mother left home is unclear to her or anyone. There are many people who are going through the same thing. Sometimes it could be from what they suffered as a child. Their parents have done something to them and they are trying to figure it out. So they do it to their children. Whatever the reason it will always continue a cycle.

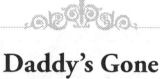

Daddy's Gone

It is late at night, and Ann is awake, she lies there in bed with tears in her eyes. Her brother Ray is lying there across the room from her in his bed. He noticed her crying, he already knows why she is crying, but he asked her anyway. She sits up and begins to talk with her younger brother about how she misses their father. He is gone and not coming back and no one knows why he just left. Abandoned by their father is just as bad as being abandoned by their mother. The sense of feeling safe and secure is a basic need that all of us have. When a child is young that is the time that his father and mother should instill their views of sense and understanding in life. The father in a child's life this time we are talking about the boys not excluding the girls this time. We are just looking at the boys because they will be the father's generation that will need guidance. It is apparent that there is a need for this, just take a look around at who is committing the crimes, young men from the inner city area mostly, who have no strong male role model in their life. If there is some way to keep them out of trouble and bring them into a proper way of being. Would they and could they listen and follow a path you set for them? Sometimes this bothers Ann at night because she wants her daddy just to be there for her. What caused her father to leave home and not return, one may never know. This has been going on for years, fathers going out to empty the garbage and not returning is one example of what I use to hear was the excuse. Just like the runaway father has no excuse to what he's done. We can guess why, but that would take all day and still we would not guess why he left. That is an individual thing on leaving.

The Bully

This story is a little hard for some of the children, because this story not only looks at the victim of bullying; it takes a look at what makes a bully.

It is late at night and Lionel, is on his way to school. Lionel is a bright and intelligent kid. He is a good student at the local middle school. The future is looks good for Lionel, but there is one thing wrong. Like clockwork, he's confronted day by day by Mike Washington, the school yard bully, who always likes bullying and intimidating Lionel. Every morning Mike ould meet Lionel down the street in front of the school, and merciless would bully Lionel in front of the other kids. The way he would talk t Lionel in front of the other kids was embarrassing. This would go after day and Lionel would tell his parents but his father would tell w when he was younger how he got bullied as well. He would tell bout how he faced down the bully and that he should be able to me for himself. Lionel then tried to tell the principal about the t often nothing would happen, just a conference between the d Lionel. Then he even went to his teachers, but they would go away. The situation had gotten so bad that it started n Lionel's school work and his behavior in school. It was what happened to Lionel. Love and protection from his parents, or the promise that his teach and principal was suppose to be giving him. It's like Lionel had said, no one cared about him and that he was just wasting time. "What have I ever done to deserve this?" Lionel would ask. He was bullied to and from school. This was getting to be too much with all this pressure mounting up on Lionel. He could not deal with it anymore. The constant bullying by Mike, and embarrassing him in front of his classmates and friends. It was early one morning when his father went to wake Lionel up to get ready for school, another day of pure hell for Lionel. But much to his surprise, Lionel was dead! Could Lionel's death been avoided? Could there have been a better way for Lionel? There were many ways this could have been handled for Lionel. He just could not see it. He could have talked to a counselor. Don't laugh, but he could have talked to a barber, a neighbor, or even Mike's family. The important thing is, he could have kept talking until someone listened. This is about eleven percent of pain that our young people have to endure. We must address this issue soon before it becomes too late.

Cyber Bullying

It is late at night and Ricky is walking around the house as he is looking at a book. This young thirteen year old is viewed by his friends as a geeky, but intelligent kid that never has a problem with anyone. Someone is bullying him by means of the internet and it has him scared. When I say scared, I mean scared. He is being cyber bullied. It is a new kind of bullying that is done over the internet, where a person is posting insulting negative remarks about another person. Rickey is staying in the house and he doesn't want to go outside. If he goes outside that someone is waiting on him and probably would get him. So he stays in the house until his mother comes home. Even then he doesn't want to go outside for long. This went on for a while until he said that he was tired and he wanted to meet the bully and they will do it after school on the playground. Well the time came for them to meet. To their surprise, it was a little kid about seven years old who had scared Ricky so bad. This is a comical look at cyber bullying, but goes to show how the aid the internet help people get away with bullying about anyone.

You're Worthless

It is late at night and James is sitting in a chair in the living room of his apartment. Sometimes he tries to shake the sound from his head, but it's still there. The voices he is hearing are the sounds of being called worthless and useless by his father. All he wanted was to be loved by his father, but all he got was abuse. This kind of abuse is far more harmful that the physical abuse, believe it or not. The number of kids that are effected by this form of abuse is staggeringly high. James had low self esteem and often made bad choices without thinking them through. James could still hear his father yelling at him and call he and his brother names at only twelve years old. He would order and boss them around as if they were nothing to him. This problem has been going on for years. James is now twenty-four years old and moved out of his father's house and has a family of his own. Sometimes, James has a problem trusting adults because when he was younger, they were the ones who mainly kept yelling at him. Like his father. Sometimes he felt like he was worthless and could do nothing right. He has a problem trusting people who have done nothing to him. James would become angry at his brother, Charles, who was verbally abused with him, especially when Charles didn't do anything. He would even try verbally abusing certain people on the job. As time went by, James would start to even take on his father's behavior with verbally abusing his family. Verbal abuse tends to hurt a person to the extinct that they can cause people to feel the effect long after the abuse stops. Like mentioned earlier, verbal abuse is more common than physical abuse, and far more harmful. Children are more acceptable to the exposure of verbal abuse, because of their age and their trust in you. You can make a child feel as if they cannot do nothing right and they are worthless. Also, it can lead to a passive behavior and allows them to be subject to bullying behavior and other times feel useless. Aggressive behaviors are also another reason you should be careful of not hurting people verbally. Making people more angry and aggressive can also lead to physical abuse too, because the fact is they are more prone to physically attacking people because they in a sense had enough verbal abuse and like Popeye, "Enough is Enough and I can't stand no more." Then they would lash out.

Lonely Angela

It is late at night and Angela is getting ready for bed. As Angela is getting ready for bed, her father yells out to her, "Hurry to bed, you have a busy day tomorrow at school." As Angela hurries her father looks back over his like through Angela's life. He thinks back to when he was eleven years old and how hard it was for him to go to school and mingle with the other kids, but they would often laugh at him because he is a white kid going to a predominately black school and they made fun of the clothes he wore. It was so hard of a mentality for him that at times he would not go to school. He just would try to make up an excuse, but his mother was not buying it, she just simply made him go to school. He would sometimes try to make friends by clowning. That was not going to work. This followed him to adulthood and that is why he doesn't allow Angela to have any friends. They can't even call to talk with her on the phone not even for a few minutes. He just won't allow her any contact with the outside world. This would sound like he is over protective, but he is not. He is just keeping her away from the outside world, because he did not trust it. A few years later, Angela is now twenty-one years old and she is a mother of two boys, one is two years old and the other is a one year old. It seems that Angela, like others who are sheltered at a young age, when she got a taste of freedom; she went wild, because of her father's fear. He just wanted to do what he felt was right, by keeping her locked away from society. This is a wide spread practice of most parents, to keep their children away from society. As they learn most of the time when the children grow up and get away, they can't cope with society and problems may it may bring. They don't know how to deal with it, they just cope with it the best they know how. Usually, they go with the flow. They try to mingle in. If Angela's father would have known how to let Angela go out just a little bit at a time and got to know Angela's friends and monitor her from afar, maybe things would have turned out diffently for Angela. What could have been done? Sometimes he could have just had a simple little talk with her and allowed her to express how she's feeling, but he just did not because he didn't know how to. This is a form of abuse that is not that commonly heard of but it does exist. A lack of not expressing yourself is like what Angela and her father experienced. The lack of the ability to express themselves or tell anyone how they feel, often leads to them acting out or living their lives out in a way that you cannot predict or control.

Lonely Tommy

It is late at night and Tommy's mother was always hard on him about staying in school and going to college. She felt that would make him a better person and give him a chance to make it in life and he would not end up like the rest of them. Who was she talking about? The others she was referring to, was the neighborhood. Why does she feel this way about the neighborhood? It's because they lived in a rough neighborhood and she graduated from college and tends to look down on people that did not go to college or finish college. She felt like that was an excuse and that they were good at excuses and that is why they were going nowhere. Tommy often felt that it was because his father did not go to school and he was able to get her pregnant and the two did not want to get married. Sometimes Tommy wondered if she was just taking her anger out on him, by punishing him. Either case she had Tommy, and she was going to make sure he was going to be somebody in life. Tommy would come home from school at the time she designated for him. If he came home anytime later, the punishment was severe. He too, always completed his homework, and kept his room immaculate. Still he was not allowed to have friends. Whenever she would go out she treated him special, compared to the other kids that she would keep every now and then. When Tommy would ask her if he could spend the night over a friend's house, she would respond in a argumentative way. She would just end with saying no. This was life for him, until Tommy grew up and left home the ripe age of eighteen years old and he never bothered to return, only to visit, but not to stay. At nineteen years old, he became a father and at twenty-one years old, he dropped out of school and got a job at a local warehouse. All he knows was that in spite of all that he was going through, he was happy. He's not going back to where he came from. This feels like I was peeking in your bedroom window when you were growing up, but I was not. It is just the way that many people I grew up in life with were and became. This too is a form of abuse that many Americans go through.

Why Can't They Get Along?

It is late at night and Kathy is getting ready to go over her father's house. He will be over in the morning so she hurries at getting her things together. Her eleven year old mind wonders why her parents are not together like they were once before. They could be a normal family once again, if they would just try. They just did not because they were determined to end their marriage. They were so much in a hurry and arguing to the end, that they did not pay attention to Kathy's feelings. This would make her feel so sad that sometimes, she would cut herself on the arm. This would make her feel somewhat fee and it tends to ease the pain she was in mentally, and it also provided an escape. If they could not be normal parents, then she did not have to be a normal child. This is a form of self mutilation; it is a rare form of abuse. It is when a person takes a knife or some sharp object and they find relief or even some form of sexual gratification. That is normal for children of divorced kids; they just don't understand why their parents can't get along with each other like they do on television. This form of self abuse id a rare form of abuse, but it is abuse. Why can't they always get together and talk the situation out. There we have a perfect ending, but it is just not like that. Kathy can't understand why. So she just abuses herself, by cutting herself. Sometimes when you, as children, are witnesses to your parent's divorces, you have to understand that the fighting is between them, not between you and your parents. It is hard to accept your parents going through a divorce. There are times that you feel like they are working it out, but they are not. They just can't get along together anymore and feel like it's better if one of them should leave and the other should stay behind to raise the child. Sometimes they bother can raises the child, but from different homes. They have to be understanding to their children. This is most unpleasant for children like Kathy. There sat her down after finding out about her problem and reassured her that they still loved her and nothing would come before her. To reassure a child that you still love them makes them feel more loved and secure. They would likely do better in school and life. Not taking time to talk to a child about the divorce makes them feel as if they have done something wrong and probably would cause them to feel worthless and start them on a life of crime.

I Hate Myself

It is late at night and Antonio is at a tattoo shop getting yet another tattoo on his arm. The tattoo is a symbol of his anger and rage that he feels. Why does he feel so much anger and who is it that he's so angry towards? It started with his father first. Often when his father comes home on the weekend he is normally drunk and he would always start in on his mother with and argument. Then there were times she would argue with his father for apparently no reason. She just starts in on him for no reason. This always seems to provoke Antonio, who was eleven when they started yelling and cursing at each other. He just wanted them to stop and try to talk with each other, but they won't and it is this that drives him crazy mad. When Antonio was fourteen years old, he came home with a tattoo on his left arm. It was a tattoo of a skull. This made Antonio's parents so mad that they began to argue with him. It is unusual to hear them fussing at him instead of each other. When they finally felt like they had got to him, the next day they began to argue with each other again and not Antonio. After a while they would began to argue and would pay Antonio little to no attention at all. So again Antonio came home with another tattoo that he proudly was showing off to his parents. This would enrage them and once again, they started arguing and fussing at him. Once again, he felt that he was the center of attention. Then when it was over, they would start back to fighting amongst themselves. They would begin an argument with each other and again he would get another tattoo. This would continue on for quite some time, he getting tattoos and then there were other things, such as stealing and drugs. Until finally, at nineteen years old, his parents asked him to leave home and he had no place to stay. That was not their problem, they were tired of him and his little stunts, so they put him out. This form of self mutilation often goes unnoticed amongst the parents and other individuals.

Don't Give Up On Your Dreams

It is late at night and Terry is up and writing songs. His parents often would tell him that he does not have what it would take to be a song writer, and that writers are born with the ability to do this. They don't know what writing songs is what Terry has always wanted to do. It is as if he was born to do this all his life. To not trust or believe your child can be a horrible experience for a child. Try seeing how it feels when someone tells you that you are not good at something and they just put you down. In Terry's parents mind, they did not know they were putting him down; they just did not want to see Terry make a dummy out of himself. Why they couldn't just simply encourage him instead of discouraging him? This is a form of abuse that is very similar to verbal abuse, not the kind that is making a child feel worthless. It is the type where a child needs your support and not you putting them down. Like Terry's parents, instead of encouraging him like they should, they put him down. They felt as though, Terry would just get a job working and that would be that. Often Terry would have felt better if he would have just had his family or somebody that would stand behind him and encourage him. Instead they talked Terry into working at a neighborhood grocery store. One can make it if someone believe in you and you believe in yourself. To believe in a child is like believing in yourself. It is like you can do almost anything you set your mind to, by believing in a child not just your child but a child who needs you and your belief in them. If you want to be a part of someone's life and make a happy ending for a child, try believing in a child.

Why Can't I?

It is another Saturday night and once again Ray, a fifteen year old student at a local middle school was at home feeling depressed that he had done nothing as usual. Maybe it's because every time he tries to do something like playing football, basketball, or sing in the choir or anything that was considered good, his friends would laugh at him. Despite what the coaches said or the choir instructor said in an effort to discourage him and it worked. He often would feel discouraged and he would quit doing whatever he was doing so that people would stop laughing and talking about him. That was when he was fifteen years old. A few years have gone by and now Ray, a twenty-one year old, and still unable to make up his mind on doing something without some kind of negative feedback, it's because he is scared of getting laughed at. One day he saw one of his old friends named Mike, he was one of the friends that use to make fun of Ray, and he is coming out of the store. As they were talking, Mike told Ray about how he wished he had the opportunity that Ray had. Ray was curious about how Mike could have been so envious of him and asked what opportunity he had. "A lot" said Mike, he said that Ray had all types of opportunities to better himself. "I don't know why you did not take any of them". This is odd because he was one of the kids who teased him and often made him feel useless. What he did not know is that Mike was actually envious of him and deep down, he wanted to be like Ray and have the opportunity that Ray had and so were others. It was as if he was some kind of a hero. Ray began to feel kind of good about himself, but why they did not tell him this when he was going through it. What he would have done just to hear his friends say that they were supporting him and they like what he was doing. This would have made such a major impact on him. A lot of it had to do with Ray's being rich. I'm taking about financially rich. It was something pretty, but that is what it was all about. "Why can't I get a break?" It is that attitude with most Americans are going through. Like I said on the previous story, you can do almost anything you want when you believe in yourself.

It Is Always My Fault

We are now in the home or Robert Smith. He is a sixteen year old worker at a local grocery store where he is a store clerk. Often, he would try to do his best to keep people happy, and to desperately be liked by everyone. He would sometimes fall sort and this would make him angry and sad because he does not know how to feel. It is easy to see that he has low self esteem when everybody's always yelling at him and always holding him responsible for whatever went wrong. It has been this way every since Robert was a little boy. Everyone blames him for something that was not his fault, especially his father who did not take any excuses that he made. It was like that all of his life. Everyone always blamed and yelled at him for something he did not know about. It went on that way for years. After a while whenever he was asked to do something, he would tell them what he knew of the situation or just do it and then he would go on as if they did not say anything to him and sometimes he would get away with blaming him things that they were responsible for. This does not seem to bother Robert, but there is little he can do about it. Is it because he has been letting people do him like this his whole life and he did not try to stop it? This is a form of verbal abuse that can carry on and have had a long consequence. He lays there at night, thinking about it. This form of abuse is an emotional abuse that has affected untold amounts of Americans and many more will be affected.

Wanda's Story

It is night time, and Wanda is up getting a baby bottle ready for her baby.

Wanda was a bright and intelligent young lady, who always had a bright look on the future. She was only sixteen years old when she started to get involved with a twenty-five year old name Joe, who was a local thug in their neighborhood. It all started when Wanda was walking home from school and Joe approached her. He was quite charming to her as he was talking to her. They talked for what seemed like hours, but it was only a few minutes. Joe asked Wanda for her phone number, and without hesitation she gave it to him and told him what time she would be home. Later that night, Joe called and again they started back talking. It was later on when he asked her to have sex with him. At first, she hesitated, "You barely know this person," she was thinking to herself. A few more seconds went by and he issued a sarcastic threat, by asking her was she scared. "No" she answered. "Well do you want to get together and do something?"

"Okay" she said. Little did she know that was going to begin a downward spiral for her. Yes she slept with Joe for awhile, and then they broke up from seeing each other. Now she is dating one of his friends and they are already sleeping around. She has a baby by another friend of his that she was sleeping with. She does not see anything wrong with it. There are a lot of things wrong with it. She doesn't realize that she is just being passed around from one to the other for fun not love. This is one form of abuse that a lot of mothers don't take into consideration. They have to start talking more to their daughters about sex and the little games that people play. The number of girls that fall victim to these little games are just outstandingly high.

If Only I Would Have Thought About It

It is night and Kevin is sitting alone in a dark room. The young twenty-two year old was sitting thinking about what had happened. "How did I get caught messing with her?" "I mean all I did was got me a little and that was it." "How did it come to this?" It all started with a simple call to his house by Karen, one of his younger sister's friends. She was wondering if Alice was at home. "No," he said, while he was sitting in the back chair to talk with her some more. As the two of them continued talking, he realized that there was something here. He could probably get her to come over and see what would happen. Karen was wondering too if they could get together and see what would happen. The only problem was that she was sixteen years old. Would that be a problem she was wondering? He said no it wouldn't. "I won't tell if you won't," Kevin said. "Karen how long will Alice be gone and who is at home with you?" "Alice is over Lorie's house, you and I both know she will be over there for a while," said Karen. "So how about it, Can you come over or are you scared?" said Kevin. Karen did not say anything, she just hung up the phone, and a few minutes later, there was a knock at the door. It was Karen, and she had on some rather skimpy looking clothes. As Kevin let her in, he was looking around to make sure that she was not being followed. You know what else happened. This went on for a while; they would meet at his house for a liaison. Then they would go their separate ways and Kevin did not mind that. All he wanted was to get him some and keep on going. It was that way until Karen got wind that Kevin was telling everybody about their little meetings. He also was telling everyone that she was nothing but a little freak on the side. She became angry and said "I've got to get him back somehow." You know the old saying about hell has no fury like a woman scorned? She then set a plan that was simple into place. All she had to do is catch him in the act and that was what she did. It was oh so easy to set him up and he agreed to it, but this time it was record tape video on her phone. Kevin was indicted on the charges and now sits there in a jail cell wondering what happened and why.

Carroll's Story

It has been a long day for Carroll. She is tired and all she wants is a hot bath and to lay down and fall asleep. That sounds like a winner, but there is one problem.

She just can not do it, because in her mind he will come back and haunt her in her dreams like he usually does. Who is it that keeps haunting Carroll's dreams? She dreams about her son Martin, who she misses so much, but she knows in her heart she will never see Martin again. Carroll closes her eyes and tries to sleep for a few minutes. It works, but just a few minutes. It was when Martin was a six year old boy playing in the front yard at their home back in Kansas City, Missouri. Martin was playing a game of catch with one of his friends Eric from down the street. He is laughing aloud and having fun. He yells out to his mother, "Look Mom, I caught a ball." Carroll whom is sitting in the front room covered in thick smoke yells out, "That's nice." She then goes back to smoking her marijuana with her girl friends that she has over. They then go back to their conversation without paying much thought to it and smoking drugs. That was a usual day for Carroll. It didn't matter much to her, because just like most mothers in America, she was raising her child alone and she did not think that smoking a little marijuana now and then would hurt. It was like that until that day came. It started off just as other days would, her friends came over and they gathered in the living room of the house. As the smoke filled the room and the laughter begins to start up they would start chattering. That went on for a little while until a knock at the door came. It was at that time a loud siren came blasting down the street. The knock at the door became louder, more intense, and with a voice yelling out loud, "Carroll, its Martin!" When she heard that it was Martin, Carroll staggered to her feet, tried to answer the door. As she staggers out of the house, she runs down the street. He was not suppose to be out of the yard, he knew this, but why would he go down the street to see what's wrong. As she arrived on the scene, she approached an officer. As she approaches him, she identifies herself as his mother. That's when the officer told her the news that no mother wanted to hear. Carroll later was taken into custody for drugs. She later thinks about how if she wasn't getting high she could have been watching out for her son and he never would have been killed.

Angela

It is night time and Mitchell is walking up to his daughter's grave site. He kneels down and starts crying. After a while he stops crying and sits there and he lets his mind drift back to when his daughter was only one year old. That is when he was at his happiest. He had Angie, who was seventeen years old girlfriend and Angela, his one year old daughter. Mitchell was still young and thought like a young man would after all he was only twenty one years old and like I said he was at his happiest. Every now and then he wanted to go outside of the relationship, come back to Angie and still have a good relationship. This sounded good to Mitchell, but not to Angie, she did not like that. She knew that every now and then, Mitchell would go out and see other women. Why he had to see other women? He would just ignore the question and continue ona s if she didn't say anything. It was that way until one day Angie had enough and decided to leave and she took Angela with her. Mitchell was disappointed at first, but he got use to it and soon he was dating again. Angie would let him come over to see Angela whenever he wanted to see her. Sometimes, she would let him take her home with him. This went on daily, until one day Mitchell received a phone call, it was Angie. She was telling him it's Angela, and he needed to come over quick. A he was on his way all kinds of thoughts were racing through his mind, but nothing could prepare him for what had happened. Squad cars, ambulances, and police officers were standing around ain in the midst ofit all, he saw Angela. She was lying there lifeless and bleeding from the left side of her head. Angie came running up to Mitchell, she was crying and yelling "Our little angel Angela, she is gone she is gone!" "What happened," Mitchell asked again. "I don't know, I heard a lot of noises and realized it was gun shots. When I ran out to get her, it was too late." The shooters were never caught. Angela's tombstone is all they have to remind them of her along with feelings of guilt to this young couple. Need we talk about this in America?

The Gun

It is late at night and little Johnnie is sitting in a police station answering questions that are being thrown at him. There are a lot of questions being thrown at the little nine year old. What happened and how it happened. That was an interesting question, what did happen? Johnny's father was an armed security officer and he worked at a local bank. He always brought his gun home at the end of the day. He would sneak down to his room and store the gun in the closet. He would then go back and join the rest of the family on their daily events. It was that way for him and his family for a while, until one Saturday evening Johnny was sitting around the house watching television, as he normally would do. That is when his older brother, Jimmy, had come into the room and said to Johnny, "Come here, I want to show you something." So Johnny went to see what it was Jimmy wanted to show him. So as Johnny came quietly into the room Jimmy quietly reached into the closet and pulled out their father's gun. He was showing it to Johnny and marveling at it when the gun accidentally went off. The noise scared Johnny at first and when he had calmed down he said "Jimmy, wow that's loud!" When Jimmy did not answer Johnny called out to him again, while looking towards the area Jimmy was last seen standing. That's when Johnny got the surprise of his life. Jimmy was lying then in a puddle of blood and he was not moving. Johnny ran and hid in his bedroom until his parents came home. Children die about 400 times a year as a result of weapons that they have found.

Gena's Story

It is late at night and the Smith's are returning home from a destination that all parents don't want to go to. It was to the hospital, to identify Gena, their seven year old daughter. What had happened? What could be so bad that Gena had to be transported to the hospital? The story begins with her mother, a single mother or two who brought home a gun. The news was so exciting to her about her mother bringing home a gun. She was telling her older brother about it and where her mother had hid it. Tim, her seventeen year old brother, was afflicted with a local street gang in the neighborhood. He felt that having a gun would make him a little tougher than normal and get him the respect that he felt was owed. The day came when their mother brought home the gun. Gena was excited as most kids would be. Gena's mother then hid the gun, a shiny new .32 caliber, under the bed in a shoe box. She told Gena not to touch the gun or tell anybody where the gun was. Gena, like most kids said she was not going to tell anybody, but we know better than that. As soon as their mother left the house Gena hurried to her brother's room and told him that the gun is here and where their mother hid it. Tim came into the room to see the gun. Tim was marveling at the beauty of the gun and how good it felt holding it in his hand. He put the gun back into the box. Later on when he was alone, Tim came back into the room and took the gun out of the box. He was going to show his gang the new gun and how he was going to use it to intimidate the other kids with it. He did not see Gena when she came into the room and he did not know that the gun was loaded. Gena scared him and he turned around stunned and pulled the trigger shooting Gena in the stomach. Gena fell down to the ground holding her stomach, because she was bleeding. "Gina!" Tim yelled out in shock. When his mother returned home, she was surprised to see an ambulance loading a body and police cars standing around in the midst of them. "Tim!" she cried, while running to him. "What happened, where is Gena?" Again, this is what happens when parents leave guns lying around and kids can find them.

Let's Get Drunk

It is late at night and Tyrone is coming out of AA rehab for the second time in his sixteen year old life. He has been drinking off and on for three years. It started when he was thirteen years old and in the seventh grade. Thomas was his best friend, they often walked to school together, Stanley is Thomas's older brother, and he's an upper classman who normally doesn't associate with students in grades lower than his. What was unusual about this day was that Stanley was at home getting ready for school; his mother had already gone to work. Tyrone came over and was waiting for Thomas, Stanley came into the room laughing and asked Tyrone if he wanted to stay home from school and drink holding up a bottle of Jack Daniels that he had hid in his room. Both Tyrone and Thomas looked at each other and said yes why not. So the two of them sat their books down and Stanley who was already slightly drunk gave them the bottle he was drinking from and was laughing as they took turns drinking from it. A few hours went by and they were drunk and boy were they stupid drunk. They had fun tearing up the house; it was that way for a while. Finally Stanley looked up at the clock and said "Mom will be back soon, let's clean up." A few days later, Tyrone was back over with bottle of Jack Daniels and Thomas was not interested. Stanley didn't mind staying home to get drunk again, so they stayed home from school and got drunk. This would go on for some time until the school started to send absentees and tardy list to Tyrone's mother. That's when Tyrone began to realize that he had a problem and he needed help. He checked into Alcoholic Anonymous. It has been a hard battle for Tyrone, but he is trying. It is no secret that 75-85 percent of our children, especially high school children, have tried alcoholic beverages.

Why Don't They Give Me A Chance

It is late at night and we now are taking a look at Jamie, a seventeen year old young beautiful high school teenager. Jamie is looking out of a window and she sees nothing but an empty life staring back at her reflection in the window. I'm young, good looking, and I have a brain. She doesn't understand why life has dealt her such a hard blow. All she ever wanted was a fair chance to make it in life, but life just wasn't fair to her. It offered her two babies that she had dropped out of high school to take care of, because she could not afford a baby sitter, and her mother just could not take off of work to baby sit. She does not feel like anything is wrong when she lets her boyfriend come over and they would do drugs. She has nothing going her way, but drugs and the sell of drugs. Her boyfriend Alan, is a young high school dropout and the father of Jamie's two little boys. They just wanted to provide a home with a yard for their sons to play in. they just do not see the error of their ways. This form of abuse is when parents sell drugs in front of their children. This exposes children to the same hopeless life that their parents had. The cycle would just repeat itself over and over again.

Adam's Story

It is late at night and Adam is a quiet young man who seems to have everything going for himself and he is going to make it. As Adam is getting ready for graduation, he thinks back over his life and how it is that way. When Adam was a young man, twelve years old to be exact, he was introduced to drugs in the worse way. He was just simply playing with his friend Wallace while at school, when he stumbled onto some more friends standing behind the school house doing drugs. At first, he started to run and tell a teacher, but then at second glance it looked kind of interesting what they were doing behind the school. One of his friends had beckoned for him to come over and Adam, like a moth drawn to fire, came over. One of the boys offered him a half smoked joint to see would he smoke it and he did without hesitation. It was too easy for Adam to smoke a joint and after a while, Adam would smoke a joint whenever he could or one of his friends offered him one. Soon Adam desired something just a little stronger than a joint, and that's when his friend gave Adam some harder drugs to start off on. First it was a little cocaine and then it became just a little stronger, so it went to crack. Adam became hooked on drugs and there was no turning back for Adam. As time went by, the school started calling Adam's house asking questions about why he wasn't at school. This was when Adam's mother took a look at Adam's problem and she then placed Adam into a drug rehab. This is where we are now; you see Adam is not graduating from high school, trade school, or any other school like that, but from rehab. This is a struggle that nearly one million U.S. children go through daily.

What's Wrong With It

Once again, it is late at night, and Tina is sitting outside of her house staring at the stars aimlessly. She is deeply depressed about something, and what is it. She's pregnant again and she doesn't know how to tell her mother about it, but she is going to because she is three months pregnant and is starting to show. It is not because she wants to, but she hat to because she is living at home with her mother. It does not make any sense at all. All she wanted to do was to have some fun, but it should not be so hard of a punishment for a little fun. She is thinking about how her mother is threatening to put her out if she gets pregnant again. "It is Ron's fault," she would say to herself. He was the one who wanted to do it, but her mother is not going to see it that way. She is right like the old saying "It takes two." None the less she sits there and ponders on what she has to do. Tina is just thirteen years old. There are 800,000 girls in America that gets pregnant and the problem is growing. Some people like Tina have sex just for the fun of it. It's just plain old sex and they feel like nothing is wrong with it.

Eddie's Story

It is late at night and Eddie, and eighteen year old, has been drinking on the same beer for what seems to be for hours. All day long it seems like that is all he wants to do is suck on a beer. From the time he gets up, until time he goes to bed. It is the same thing every day. There was nothing to do but suck on a bottle or drink out of a can of beer. It is like that's all he went to school for. This is the life of Eddie and his neighborhood. There is nothing going on and to no one has a job, they just come home and sit on their behinds and wait for his mother to come home so he could borrow some money from her, money that he knows he will never pay back. This sound familiar doesn't it, always borrowing from someone with no intentions of paying it back at all. We all know someone like that. It is a different story when someone else is always borrowing money for all kinds of reasons and we know these people, but it doesn't make any sense to loan money to a person who just wants to drink beer all day long. What is it that makes Eddie and his friends so lazy that they just have no motivation to get up and do something with their lives? Perhaps, it is because drinking tends to lessen a person from making a little slower reaction. It's retards or slows down the system and makes it hard for a person to get up and get jobs or think a little slower. Whatever the case, maybe alcohol is a problem and we must take it serious.

What Are Some Problems

Some problems that can lead America's children to do what we have been discussing. Better yet, some of the problems that lead the abuser to abuse their victims.

While it is true that an abused person grows and become the abuser. That never seems to end does it? All we want is the answer to where it begins and that's all we want to know. It is unfortunate that we just cannot find it. All we know is that we are the victims and they are the ones that get to go around hurting people. It is hard to believe that the aggressor was once a victim, just as you, but their life was taken away from them by means of a brutal and selfish way. Let's take a look at some of Kelly's story. You would automatically feel that she was the one and only victim, but did anyone consider that Uncle Terry was a victim as well. Did the cycle continue on?

Class Clown

It is late at night and Arnold is sitting alone in his room thinking back over the day. He laughs at what he's done to make the class laugh at him, and now he was thinking about what he could do to make them laugh at him tomorrow. It is not unusual for people like Arnold to be concerned about making people laugh at him than he is about getting his lesson in school. To this thirteen year old it's not important to get passing grades than it is to get students to laugh at him. Why is it more important? Is it because when he gets home from school, there is no one there? That was often the case for Arnold. He would often come home to an empty house. His mother was always gone to work and if she was at home, she would often be too sleepy or too tired to take up any time with him. She did not allow him to go outside due to the fact they lived in a rough neighborhood. She was not that concerned with his grades. She just wanted him to pass his test and move on to the next grade. This is why when Arnold went to school; he found a world of people he could entertain. To him school was a world of entertainment. It was like every day he had a kingdom and it waited for his coming every morning. He enjoyed getting laughs when he was clowning with his teachers and they would take up for him if a teacher would write him up or get him suspended. Yes, it was like Arnold was a king and the school was his kingdom. It was that way until Arnold was transferred to another school where no one knew him. He had to start over again. This is a form of neglect that most parents are guilty of, but they don't know that they are. The child just wanted to spend a little time with them, but the parents just don't know.

Class Cut Up

It is late at night and Francis is sitting in her room looking out of her window. She's thinking about how she is going to get Mrs. Edwards, her 7th grade English teach, back for having her suspended. This is why she is in the room alone, because her mother abuses her. For example, she would get yelled at and whipped, along with all other types of punishments that her mother deemed worthy for her. Maybe it seemed abusive to her and sometimes the abuse was unnecessary, but he endured it. She always got upthe next morning and went to school. She would take out her feelings by being a class cut up. She was good at doing that in all of her classes, except Mrs. Edwards's English class. It seemed that Mrs. Edwards was on to her every move. At times she would beat Francis at her moves. This was starting to get on Francis's nerves that she could not beat Mrs. Edwards at anything. To Francis,, it was like she was reading her mind and knew what she was going to do before she did it. This went on for the whole school year, and then there came the day that Francis tired and defeated, asked Mrs. Edwards calmly, "What is it that I have done to you?" Mrs. Edwards calmly explained to Francis that she hasn't done anything. "I recognized the symptoms of abuse and I know that somewhere along the line, you are abused and you are just acting out." This made Francis's eyes swell up, and she started to slightly cry. Mrs. Edwards then explained how she knew that Francis was being abused, because she was abused herself. At that point Francis completely broke down and lost it, she cried so bad that Mrs. Edwards had to hold her up to let her cry on her shoulder. It was some time later when Francis stopped crying and felt that she could talk to Mrs. Edwards about anything and she would talk to Mrs. Edwards regularly. Francis became close to Mrs. Edwards and in time, they became almost like friends and were inseparable. They were so tight that years later at Francis's graduation, Mrs. Edwards was there.

Sex Does Things

It is late at night and Tameka is up walking around the house getting ready for a date with Eddie, a nice looking young man, but this is not an ordinary date. It happens to be their third date and it will be the third time that she will sleep with him. It is Tameka's way of thinking that they are in love, but it is not love, it is lust. That is the way Tameka thinks every time she gets together with a young man she automatically will lay down with him. Tameka feels as though she has to sleep with her partner to keep her relationship. Why is this? She is only thirteen years old and Eddie is only fourteen years old. Some people who do not have their parents in their lives feel that by sleeping with someone it takes the place of the absent parents. If they don't stay together after they sleep together, they would just go on to the next one and try to find the love that they desperately need at home. This is a form of neglectful parenting this form normally involves when the parents don't have time for the children. The children will raise themselves the best way they can. That is the story of a lot of children in the United States. A lot of times these kids who are having sex are doing it because they need to be loved in the right way, instead of having being loved the wrong way. To be a part of their lives in the right way means a lot to the kid and it can lead to them not being so sexually active. This is the message that Tameka's parents need to hear instead of every now and then having to go out looking for Tameka from one young man's house to another young man's house.

Nothing To do

It is late at night and Eric is walking around in the front room of his apartment. He hears a knock at the door and it is Jan, she is seventeen years old and Eric is sixteen years old and they are about to have sex again. It doesn't matter to them because when they get together in his mother's house it is all about sex to both of them. It is the only fun they would have. They are living in the heart of the ghetto and the only fun they would have is sex. It is what most people in poverty think. Getting in a car and going somewhere is not an option to them. They just know sex is something they can do and from time to time, even that gets boring to them. It would help them if they had something better to do, or at least something that would keep them interested. Life like this often leads to pregnancy, not to mention HIV or aids. They just do what they do because there is no one who cares about them or at least it seems that way for them. As time went by, Eric grew bored with Jan, and now he is dating someone else by the name of June. Eric is already in love with June and they have been going together for only two weeks. They are already sleeping with each other. The cycle continued for Eric, and it will never change unless he breaks the cycle.

Dee-Dee's Love

It is late at night and Doris is waiting for Michael to bring their daughter Dee-Dee home from visiting him. He is allowed to get her every other weekend. She stands at the door of the house and waits. When Michael returns home and he lets Dee-Dee out of the car, she runs up to the house and goes into the house. Doris doesn't say a word; she just goes in the house and shuts the door. That was how their visits would end. She would then have to hear her mother complain about her father all night. She would have to listen to her talk about how her father could not do anything right. She is always in the wrong. "What can I do to make it right," the twelve year old would say to herself. That is what she asked herself every time she came home from visiting with her father. It was not that her mother hated her; it is just the fact that she has a relationship with her father and that is good. The problem is that it is not her fault. Her mother just hates her father for marrying someone other than her. This is typical, it is not unusual for a parent to hate or speak badly about a parent for marrying another. Sometimes the parent is caught up in the middle of it. When all they wanted to do was live with that particular parent, like most children do. If there was some kind of way she could let her mother know how she feels when she talks about her father and how he doesn't seem to be bothered by her comments. It seems that all her father wants to do is love Dee-Dee and that is good for now.

It's My Fault

It is late at night and Aaron is up sitting in his bed. He had just come home from visiting his mother for the weekend, since his father has custody of him. He hears his mother and father yelling and cursing at each other in the next room over what, he did not know. That is how it is when he goes over to see her. They always got into it for something. She just can't leave without having the last word. Her heart is broken because she feels that Aaron's father might have been telling him something about her. She lost custody of Aaron because she had a drug problem and it was bad. Aaron was only six years old when his father came and got him from his mother. Aaron never thought anything of having to stay at home alone while his mother was out getting drugs to get high. That was five years ago and now he is eleven years old. He still doesn't understand why they just don't get along. "Is it my fault again," wondered Aaron. "Was it something that I had said or done?" He is just the reason for their argument a means to get at each other and take out their anger towards each other. Aaron just doesn't understand why they argue so much, he just wants them to stop. Is it any way that they could stop arguing? Parents who argue in front of their children don't realize that they make the child feel that they are somehow or someway responsible for the argument. It is not their fault, but try telling it to the child when their parents are in the middle of an argument.

Stop Yelling

It is getting late in the night and Al is walking around the house in a daze and talking to himself trying to forget all the yelling they did to him. It was about seven years ago when he was thirteen years old. All his mother did was yell at him and his brother for everything they did. She would constantly yell at them for any and everything they did wrong. What she did not know is that by yelling at them it could lead to kids who grow up into adulthood suppressing their feelings until a later date and time. They will slowly begin to act out the feeling that they have towards their parents or the person who they are mad at. It is no wonder that there is much arguing and fighting that happens. Everything starts at home even the bad things that a person does. Most of the time a person who got yelled at as a child can handle it without any problems. They are not the ones that I am concerned about. I am writing this book for the ones who can't control their anger. The ones who are trying to deal with what happened to them with all the yelling that they had to put up with, they are the ones I am writing about. It is a shame that they and to go through what they went through in order to get themselves heard. Being yelled at for any little thing, made them feel helpless and often frightened most of the time. Their mother did not care about any of that, she cared about what they did what and if yelling at them was going to get some results, then so be it. It is now seven years later, and Al is now a grown man of twenty one years, he has someone special in his life, a girlfriend by the name of Candice and to him things are going alright, but it's not going alright for him. You see, sometimes Al gets angry and starts to yell at Candice. There are times he would hit her and apologize for it, but he just can't help it. It would happen again and again until one day Al can't take it no more and he snapped. Candice will never yell at All again because she is dead. Al is now wondering what the judge will say and how much time he will get while he awaits his time in jail.

Counseling

It is late at night and Steve is on his way to his counseling class. It is a part of his weekly schedule for the past eight years, since he was twelve years old. He always would have to put up with his father yelling at him, his mother, and his little sister who is only five years old. It still bothers Steve because it was brought on by generally nothing; he just came home and yelled at them. Their father works at the local Steel Factory, and he works long and hard hours. When he comes home to his family, he takes out his anger on them by yelling and cursing. After a while he then slowly started with the hitting him, his mother, and his sister. The yelling continued and the hitting then became beatings, for no reason at all, even when they did everything right. He still would come home yelling and beating on them for no reason at all. This yelling that he did, plus the occasional beatings started to terrify Steve and Elise, his little sister. Sometimes their mother would take them over their aunt's house to spend the night or weekend if they could. Then she would bring them back home to that hell hole that she called home. Sometimes they would begin to notice the changes in him, when he said things would change, and that he would do better. After a while, he would start back yelling and sometimes hitting again. This went on for years well into their adulthood. After a while they began to think it was normal. Over the years, Steve would start yelling at people whenever he got mad. Elise would let her boyfriend yell at her or she would try to get him angry enough to yell at her. This is directly because of their father yelling at them. Over time, yelling for Steve became hitting whoever he was dating and Elise would let her boyfriend hit her because that was the way she felt and what she expected. It wasn't until Steve had realized that he and his sister needed some help and he got it through counseling. Now he and his father are going to counseling.

Obesity

Obesity can be defined as excessive weight gain:

It is late at night and Shawn is stopping at a drive through restaurant where she orders a triple beef sandwich with a large fry and drink. She plans on finishing it with a cherry pie. There is no reason why Shawn has gained so much weight and everybody is teasing her about it. They don't know that Shawn is hiding something that has bothered her for years. When she was eight years old, she got raped. Her mother knew about it and she did everything she could to help her cope. It just wasn't enough weight to her, but she was just unhappy. She just wants simply decided to eat away that horrible memory she has. Obesity can be a form of self abuse. It can stem from any number of things that have happened to a person in the past. They would just hide the pain by eating food and gaining weight. He does not care about her weight gain all she wants to do is eat and forget what happened to her. Over the years Shawn had blown up to 325 lbs and it still doesn't bother her. Even when she hears other people laughing at her or under their breath talking about her, she doesn't mind. She just keeps on doing what it is that she is doing, eating a triple beef sandwich with her French fries and large cola and hot cherry pie. As she drives off into the dark eating and trying to forget the past.

It is late at night and Shelly is up and walking around the room and thinking about her baby. "My baby, where is my baby, I just want to see my baby." Shelly would say every now and then. Why she could not see her baby was that she was in the psychiatric ward of the local hospital. She was in the mental hospital for a nervous breakdown from being teased about her size. This has been an ongoing advent her entire life and she is only sixteen years old. It started when Shelly was seven years old; she used to get into fights at school with other students. When the school would request a meeting with her mother, she would come up to the school clear the suspension and leave. When she attempted to talk to her mother about the students teasing her, she would tell her that it's nothing but childhood playing and then they would go. A few years went by and Shelly was still enduring the abuse that she had to put up with. It was not until she had turned fourteen years old when she met an older man that was twenty-one years old. At first they were just talking as friends, but then as time went by, they started to become more than friends. They discussed having a baby at first, she said no, but then she thought about it and how horrible the people she came around treated her. So she agreed to have a baby. After a few months went by and arguing with her parents for getting pregnant she finally had the baby. It was a girl and Shelly was happy to have her. She had someone who she could share her love with and someone whom she could love. It did not bother her when the father ran out on her, she had somebody to love. Though she had a child and felt love the other kids still picked on Shelly and had fun doing it, but it was not fun to Shelly. One day while she was going to school one of the boys that went to school with her was teasing at her and she just did not feel like taking any mess off of anybody that day. He just kept on with taunting her. Until she finally had enough and started into him she kept hitting him and saying that she had enough and could not take anymore. This went on even after the principal tried to calm her down. It was just that Shelly could not take anymore of being teased, because of her obese size and she had a small breakdown. It wasn't until later that night when she calmed down.

Just Like Dad

A lie: Is giving a false statement or telling somebody something that is not true.

It is late at night and Emily is putting up her clothes for the seventh time. She is disappointed about her father not coming to get her. She is not okay with it, but over the years she will get use to it. It is like that almost all the time. Sometimes her father would come through and pick her up to go over his house every blue moon. Why does her father always tell her that he's going to do something, and then he doesn't? It is not that unusual that her father tells her lies and so does other fathers across the United States. Why do they lie? It's simple; most parents find it easier to lie to their children than to tell them the truth. What is amazing is that most children can handle the truth about whatever, but their parents (don't trust them) and so they lie to them. It is also hard to imagine that some parents want to hide certain things from their kids. What is so amazing is that they will find out anyway about what it is you were trying to hide from them. Whatever the case is, Emily's father would just lie to her about coming over to pick her up and she would just be left sitting out waiting on him. Eventually Emily had begun to lie just like her father did whenever she got into trouble. It was hard at first, but then it became easier and easier to lie. Emily's lies got so bad that her school had written her mother a request to speak with her about Emily and her lies. Emily would rush home from school and take the call and then lie to the school and tell them that her mother was gone and would not be home until later. They finally got in touch with Emily's mother. The fact that her father passed it down to Emily, that lying is easier than telling the truth. It did not help Emily, she was becoming just like her father, a habitual liar.

Just Cleaning The Room

It is late at night and Helen a thirteen year old is walking about the apartment cleaning the rooms. She looks back at her mother who seemed to not care about what she does. It seemed that her mother was always regretting her life that she had lived. It was as though she never got a chance to live her life at all because she had Helen. It was not Helen's fault that she was born, it was her mother's fault. Instead of worrying about a singing career that she had that could have been a great one. She was worried about keeping up with her boyfriend James, who did not care about her singing career. All he wanted to do is sleep with her and move on to the next one. She just could not see it. She just wanted to keep him, so she got pregnant by him. Well like most girls who tried to keep a boyfriend that did not work. So she had to have the baby. That is where she is today. As Helen sweeps the floor her mother would walk by her as if Helen was not there. In her mind it was all Helen's fault that they are not together and her dreams of being a star. This type of abuse is known to ignore a person's needs such as to love or beloved is like telling them that you don't want to be with that person. Yes, it is hard for Helen to accept the fact that she is not wanted, but she can live with that she has no choice but to live with it. Her mother on the other hand, she just lived. It is sad that we don't realize that this is a form of abuse. They can't help to want but never can have is what they feel and they take out their anger on who or what they said that caused them from getting there. Meanwhile, Helen just goes on with cleaning the room.

Name Calling

It is late at night and Phyllis thinks of all the names she was called out and it hurts her. The names they called her were not as hurtful as to who was calling her the names. They were supposed to have been her friends, but they talked like they were her enemies instead of her friends. This always happens to children who are getting into it with each other for various reasons. Is it abuse? No not really, it is not abuse it is just teasing. In time Phyllis would get over it. Name calling can be hurtful to other people that you don't know. Sometimes when you call a person a name that you don't think is offensive, but to them or someone nearby who is listening, you have called that person something offensive and degrading although that was not your intent to offend them. Some cutlers have certain names that they do not see as offensive as long as they are saying it to one another, but soon as you or someone else say it, that's an offensive remark that you made and did not have to make. The remarks or name calling that Phyllis had to endured also comes from the fact that they lived in a cultural environment where name calling was nothing uncommon for them to hear. It was an excitable thing to hear people calling each other names, but you would just have to be careful of the name calling and who you call a name that isn't yours.

About The Author

Gregory Sanders has had twelve years as a police officer for the city of Memphis, where he has seen a lot of these problems and he can see the solutions that can be made with some of these problems. Also, he has worked as a volunteer in the schools and was very effective solving some of the problems.

Printed in the United States
By Bookmasters